Once Upon a Time

Jaap Tuinman

CONSULTANTS
Sharon Anderson
Elaine Baker
Maxine Bone
Jill Hamilton
Diana Hill
Orysia Hull
Sandy Johnstone
Moira Juliebö
Beverley Kula
Helen Langford
Mary Neeley
Barbara Park
Carol Pfaff
Sharon Rich

PROGRAM EDITOR
Kathleen Doyle

GINN

Ginn Publishing Canada Inc.

JOURNEYS

Once Upon a Time
Anthology Level Four

© Copyright 1990 by
Ginn Publishing Canada Inc.
ALL RIGHTS RESERVED.

EDITOR
Anne MacInnes

EDITORIAL CONSULTANT
Nicki Scrimger

ART/DESIGN
Sandi Meland Cherun/
Word & Image Design Studio

C99142
ISBN 0-7702-1712-5

Printed and bound in Canada.

BCDEFGH 97654321

Acknowledgments

For kind permission to reprint copyrighted material, acknowledgment is hereby made to the following:

E.P. Dutton for "Puppy and I" from *When We Were Very Young* by A.A. Milne. Copyright © 1924 by E.P. Dutton, renewed 1952 by A.A. Milne. Reprinted by permission of the publisher, Dutton Children's Books, a division of Penguin Books USA Inc.
Harcourt Brace Jovanovich, Inc., for "Three Bears Walking" from *The Three Bears Rhyme Book,* copyright © 1987 by Jane Yolen, reprinted by permission of Harcourt Brace Jovanovich, Inc.
Clarion Books/Ticknor & Fields for *Come to the Meadow* by Anna Grossnickle Hines, copyright © 1984 by Anna Grossnickle Hines. Reprinted by permission of Clarion Books/Ticknor & Fields: A Houghton Mifflin Company.
Dial Books for Young Readers for *Turtle Tale* by Frank Asch. Copyright © 1978 by Frank Asch. Reprinted by permission of the publisher.
The Putnam Publishing Group for *We Were Tired of Living in a House* by Liesel Moak Skorpen, text copyright © 1969 by Liesel

Contents

Out and About

— from *The Mice and the Clockwork Bus,* written and illustrated by Rodney Peppé

7

Puppy and I

by A.A. Milne
Illustrated by Mireille Levert

I met a Man as I went walking;
We got talking,
Man and I.
"Where are you going to, Man?" I said
(I said to the Man as he went by).
"Down to the village, to get some bread.
Will you come with me?" "No, not I."

I met a Horse as I went walking;
We got talking,
Horse and I.
"Where are you going to, Horse, today?"
(I said to the Horse as he went by).
"Down to the village to get some hay.
Will you come with me?" "No, not I."

I met a Woman as I went walking;
We got talking,
Woman and I.
"Where are you going to, Woman,
  so early?"
(I said to the Woman as she went by).
"Down to the village to get some barley.
Will you come with me?" "No, not I."

I met some Rabbits as I went walking;
We got talking,
Rabbits and I.
"Where are you going in your brown
   fur coats?"
(I said to the Rabbits as they went by).
"Down to the village to get some oats.
Will you come with us?" "No, not I."

I met a Puppy as I went walking;
We got talking,
Puppy and I.
"Where are you going this nice
  fine day?"
(I said to the Puppy as he went by).
"Up in the hills to roll and play."
"I'll come with you, Puppy," said I.

Beeny's Bike

by Christel Kleitsch
Illustrated by Philippe Béha

Watch it! Hold on tight!
Beeny was trying to ride
her new bike. She went
up her street to the
top of the high hill.
Then she started down.
Faster, faster, and
faster she went.
At the end
of the hill,
the bike hit
a bump.

Down went the bike and down went Beeny.
"Ow!" said Beeny.
She kicked the bike
and it rolled away.
"My bike's gone,"
said Beeny. "I'm glad."

The bike rolled around the corner and bumped into Mrs. Bernardo.

Mrs. Bernardo looked around. "What was that?" she said. But the bike was gone.

The bike rolled down the street and bumped into Fritz.

Fritz looked around. "What was that?" he said. But the bike was gone.

The bike rolled along the sidewalk and bumped into Mr. Hall.

Mr. Hall looked around. "What was that?" he said. But the bike was gone.

The bike rolled down the street and bumped into Beeny.

"My bike's back," said Beeny. "I'm glad. Now I'll try to ride it around the block."

And away went Beeny on her bike.

Three Bears Walking

by Jane Yolen
Illustrated by Sharon Matthews

Three bears walking
down the lane, down the lane.
Three bears talking,
"Do you think it's going to rain?"

Three bears walking
to the wood, to the wood.
Three bears talking,
"Pretty day!" "Pretty good!"

Three bears walking
under trees, under trees.
Three bears talking,
"Do you know where there are bees?"

Three bears walking
by a stream, by a stream.
Three bears talking,
"Pass the berries." "Pass the cream."

Three bears walking
to their den, to their den.
Three bears talking,
"Great to be back home again."

21

Come to the Meadow

*Written and illustrated
by Anna Grossnickle Hines*

"Come to the meadow, Mother.
Come to the meadow with me."

"It's full of monkey flowers and shooting stars
and little tiny buttercups."

"I can't today, Mattie. The
ground is soft and I must
plant the vegetables, pull
the weeds, and tend the
rosebushes."

"Come to the meadow, Daddy.
Come to the meadow with me."
"I saw a hoptoad down by the creek and a
pokey old turtle out taking a walk."

"I can't today, Mattie. The
snow has melted and I must
clean the cobwebs out of
the shed, take down the
storm windows, and put
up the screens."

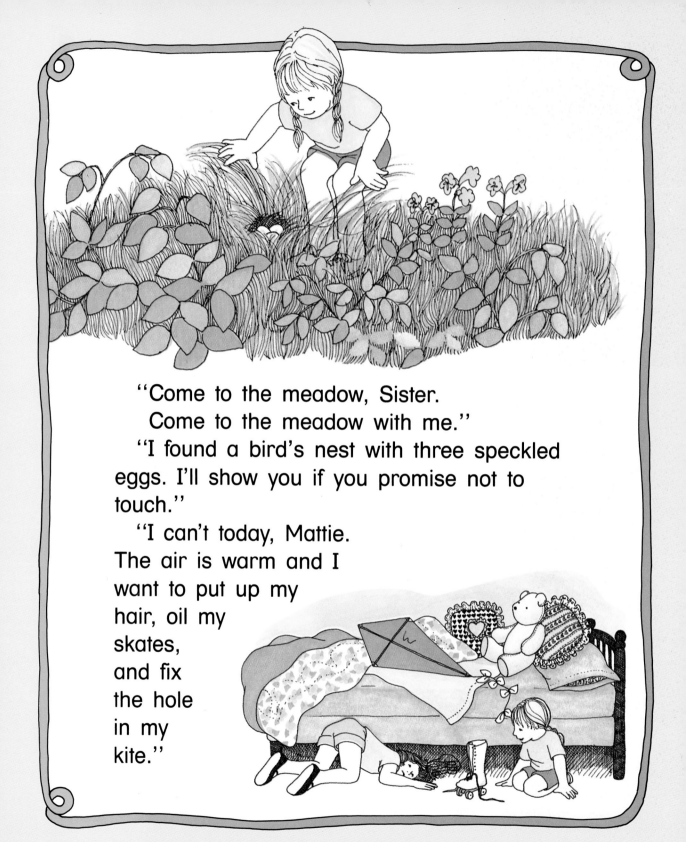

"Come to the meadow, Sister.
Come to the meadow with me."

"I found a bird's nest with three speckled eggs. I'll show you if you promise not to touch."

"I can't today, Mattie. The air is warm and I want to put up my hair, oil my skates, and fix the hole in my kite."

"Come to the meadow, Brother.
Come to the meadow with me."
"The field mice made a tunnel under the grass and the crickets are singing *cheer-up, cheer-up, cheer-up.*"
"I can't today, Mattie. The sun is shining and I have to find my baseball mitt, untangle this fishing line, and polish my bike."

"Come to the meadow, Granny.
   Come to the meadow with me."
"I saw a spider spinning
a web on a thimbleberry
bush. And the clouds
look like vanilla
ice cream."
   "In the meadow?
Spider webs and
ice-cream clouds?

Oh, let's go see and take some bread and cheese and hard-boiled eggs and apple juice . . ."
"And bananas?"
"Oh, yes, bananas."

"And cookies?"
"Especially cookies."

"And go to the meadow?"
"Straight to the meadow."

"And have a picnic?"
"Yes, a lovely,
wonderful, delicious
picnic in the meadow.

Because in the
meadow . . ."

"IT'S SPRING!"

Wake Up, Pond

Smack, smack,
  Squeak,
A mother beaver has had
3 kittens. They are blind and
are very weak.
Wake up, pond.
it's a new day.

Shona Smith

Illustrated by Andranik Aghazarian

Gulp, Gulp,
Snap
A cray fish
is swimming.
Then he said Gulp
Wake up, pond
It's a new day.

Anand Pabari

Screech, Screech,
noisy
The red - winged black bird
is feeding her babr's.
    babies
Wake up, pond,
It's a new day.

Jackie Lamport

Gulp, gulp,
Swish,
A sunfish swimming
Wake up, Pond
It's a new day.

Travis Gaeler

Turtle Tale

by Frank Asch
Illustrated by Normand Cousineau

One morning on the way to the pond an
apple fell on Turtle's head. It hurt so much that
Turtle pulled his head inside his shell and
made up his mind to keep it there, thinking,
"That's what a wise turtle would do."

Inside his shell it was so dark he couldn't see a thing. But he could still smell his way along the path to the pond.

On the way he bumped into an old friend. He bumped into rocks, fell off logs, and tumbled down hills. When Turtle got to the pond, he could neither eat nor drink. That night Turtle cried himself to sleep.

BOO HOO!

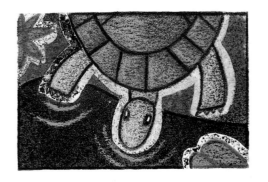

When he awoke the next morning he stuck his head out and made up his mind to keep it there, thinking, "That's what a wise turtle would do."

By then he was very thirsty and very hungry. He took a long drink . . . and had a fish for breakfast.

After breakfast he climbed on top of his favorite rock and began to sun himself. When the sun went in and raindrops began to fall, all the other animals took cover, but not Turtle!

Fox too was running for cover when he saw Turtle sunning himself in the rain, and decided to have him for lunch. While Fox leaped through the air straight for Turtle's head, Turtle thought to himself, "But then again, maybe it's best if I keep my head out sometimes and sometimes pull it . . . in."

Tucked safely inside his shell, Turtle waited for Fox to go away. When the rain stopped and the sun came out again, he finished sunning himself, thinking, "That's what a wise turtle would do."

On the Beach

by Peter Marino

An oyster has two shells joined together with a hinge. Inside is a soft body with no bones.

People collect driftwood for its beautiful shapes. Can you guess why it is called driftwood?

Did you know that seaweed is used to make medicines—and ice cream and chocolate milk?

A crab has a hard shell and two large front claws. It runs along the shore sideways!

A starfish can grow a new arm if it loses one of its arms.

Don't step on this pretty bubble on the beach. It's a jellyfish, and it can sting you!

A sand dollar is flat and has a star or flower pattern on its shell. Some people call it a *sea cookie.*

We Were Tired of Living in a House

by Liesel Moak Skorpen
Illustrated by Daniel Sylvestre

We were tired of living in a house.
So we packed a bag with sweaters and
socks and scarves and mittens and woollen
caps. And we moved to a tree. We liked
our tree.

There was always a breeze in the afternoon that rippled through our roof. Above in a branch lived a speckled bird who sang all day for the sake of a song, and our roof in the autumn turned scarlet and gold. We liked our tree,

until we tumbled out.

So we packed our bag with sweaters and socks and scarves and mittens and scarlet leaves and gold. And we moved to a pond. We liked our pond.

We built a raft and floated about among the reeds and lily pads. Below fish darted. Dragonflies above. And pond frogs sang with us on summer nights. We liked our pond,

until we sank.

So we packed our bag with sweaters and socks and scarves and scarlet leaves and gold and a frog who was a particular friend. And we moved to a cave. We liked our cave.

We slept on beds of cool green moss. We
hunted for blackberries in the woods. We dipped
our water from the brook and roasted walnuts
over a fire. When we weren't busy, we explored.
We liked our cave,

until we met the bears.

So we packed our bag with sweaters and socks and scarlet leaves and gold and a frog who was a particular friend and precious stones that caught and held the sun. And we moved to the sea. We liked the sea.

We built a castle on the shore from salty water and warm sea sand with turrets and towers and moats about. We hunted for treasure and dove in the waves and slept to the pleasant songs of the surf. We liked our castle on the shore,

but the tides kept washing us out to sea.

So we packed our bag with sweaters and scarlet leaves and gold and a frog who was a particular friend and precious stones that caught and held the sun and seashells singing like the surf.

And we went home to live in a house.

Crrack!

Photographed by Stephen Ogilvy

Chickens are birds, and so are ducks.

Chickens and ducks both lay eggs. Duck eggs are bigger than chicken eggs.

Chickens and ducks sit on their eggs to keep them warm. If the eggs get too cold, the baby birds won't hatch.

The chick and the duckling peck
at their shell with a tiny "egg tooth"
on the top of their beak. They peck
and peck and peck until
Crrrack! they hatch.

The chick and the duckling are
wet and sticky when they come out
of their shell. They have to dry
and fluff their feathers.

Now the chick and the duckling are hungry. The chick digs and pecks for something to eat.

Chicks like to eat seeds and insects. The duckling will dive into a pond to find its food. Ducklings like to eat water plants and insects.

Look at the pictures. Can you
see how the chick's feet and the
duckling's feet help the birds to
move around and find food?

The chick's feet have claws to help it walk around and scratch for bugs and worms in the ground.

The duckling's feet are webbed to help it swim in the water.

The chick and the duckling grow up. The chick grows up to be a chicken. The duckling grows up to be a duck.

How can you tell which one is the chicken and which one is the duck?

The Chick and the Duckling

by Mirra Ginsburg
Illustrated by Eugenie Fernandes

A Duckling came out of the shell.
"I am out!" he said.
"Me too," said the Chick.

"I am taking a walk," said the Duckling.
"Me too," said the Chick.

"I am digging a hole," said the Duckling.
"Me too," said the Chick.

"I found a worm," said the Duckling.
"Me too," said the Chick.

59

"I caught a butterfly," said the Duckling.
"Me too," said the Chick.

"I am going for a swim," said the Duckling.
"Me too," said the Chick.

"I am swimming," said the Duckling.
"Me too!" cried the Chick.

The Duckling pulled the Chick out.
"I'm going for another swim," said the Duckling.
"Not me," said the Chick.

Down on Grandpa's Farm

Illustrated by Laurie Stein

Chorus

Oh, we're on our way, we're on our way,
On our way to Grandpa's farm.
We're on our way, we're on our way,
On our way to Grandpa's farm.

1. Down on Grandpa's farm
   there is a big brown cow.
   Down on Grandpa's farm
   there is a big brown cow.
   The cow, she makes a sound
   like this: Moo! Moo!
   The cow, she makes a sound
   like this: Moo! Moo! *(Chorus)*

Honk! Honk!

Maa! Maa!

Moo! Moo!

Meow! Meow!

Squeak! Squeak!

Woof! Woof!

Cluck! Cluck!

2. Down on Grandpa's farm
   there is a little red hen.
   Down on Grandpa's farm
   there is a little red hen.
   The hen, she makes a sound
   like this: Cluck! Cluck!
   The hen, she makes a sound
   like this: Cluck! Cluck! *(Chorus)*

Oink! Oink!

Neigh! Neigh!

3. Down on Grandpa's farm
   there is a little white sheep.
   Down on Grandpa's farm
   there is a little white sheep.
   The sheep, he makes a sound
   like this: Baa! Baa!
   The sheep, he makes a sound
   like this: Baa! Baa! *(Chorus)*

Baa! Baa!

Quack! Quack!

63

Byron and His Balloon

by the Children of LaLoche and Friends

Byron is up and waiting.
The sun has not yet warmed the sky.
Today, he has decided,
is the day that he will fly.

One rooster crows "Good Morning"
and Byron's on his way.

2 Two farmers' trucks stand near a field,
the red one filled with hay.

3 Three women of the village
go out to wash the clothes.

4 Four chickens march most carefully,
right under Grandma's nose.

5 Five noon-hour, happy children
play ball down by the lake.

6 Six sleepy head of cattle
try hard to stay awake.

7 Seven wooden houses creak
as Byron drifts on past.

8 Eight patient pigs are waiting.
It's dinnertime—at last!

9 Nine noisy birds go flocking
towards the dying sun.

10 Ten smiling children lie in bed.
Byron counts them, one by one.

Byron's day-long flight is over.
The moon and stars appear.
"Goodbye, balloon! I thank you
for floating me back here."

Once Upon a Time

— from *The Balloon Tree*, written and illustrated by Phoebe Gilman

I Like Stories That Begin "Once upon a time"

by Naomi Shepherd
Illustrated by Mark Craig

I like these stories because they tell about kings and queens, princes and princesses, fairy godmothers and wicked giants, and all kinds of magical creatures.

I like these stories because wizards cast spells, hens lay golden eggs, frogs turn into princes, pumpkins become carriages, and anything magical can happen.

73

I like these stories because poor
people become rich, good people
win out, and bad people get punished.
But best of all, I like these stories
because they all end
"happily ever after."

The Three Billy Goats Gruff

Retold by Noella Singer
Illustrated by Michael Martchenko

Once upon a time, on a hill far away, lived three billy goats. Their names were Little Billy Goat Gruff, Middle-Sized Billy Goat Gruff, and Big Billy Goat Gruff.

One day there was no grass left on their hill. So they decided to go to another hill. But to get to that hill they had to cross over a bridge. And under that bridge lived a mean ugly terrible troll.

First came Little Billy Goat Gruff, and he went
TRIP TRAP TRIP TRAP TRIP TRAP
over the bridge.

"Who's that trip-trapping over **my** bridge?"
roared the troll.

"It is I, Little Billy Goat Gruff. I'm going up to
the hill to eat the sweet green grass."

"No you're not! This is **my** bridge, and I'm going to eat you up!"

"Oh no, please don't eat *me!* Wait for my brother, Middle-Sized Billy Goat Gruff."

"Very well, be off. I'll wait for your brother."

Then came Middle-Sized Billy Goat Gruff, and he went "TRIP" "TRAP" "TRIP" 'TRIP' 'TRAP' 'TRAP' over the bridge.

"Who's that trip-trapping over **my** bridge?"
roared the troll.

"It is I, Middle-Sized Billy Goat Gruff. I'm going
up to the hill to eat the sweet green grass."

"No you're not! This is **my** bridge, and I'm
going to eat you up!"

"Oh no, please don't eat *me!* Wait for my
brother, Big Billy Goat Gruff."

"Very well, be off. I'll wait for your brother."

Then came Big Billy Goat Gruff, and he went

"TRIP, TRAP" "TRIP, TRAP" "TRIP, TRAP"

over the bridge.

"Who's that trip-trapping over **my** bridge?" roared the troll.

"It is I, Big Billy Goat Gruff. I'm going up to the hill to eat the sweet green grass."

"No you're not! This is **my** bridge, and I'm going to eat you up!"

Up went the troll onto the bridge. Down went Big Billy Goat's horns and butted the troll. Down, down, down into the river fell the troll.

Big Billy Goat Gruff went on over the bridge

"TRIP" "TRAP" "TRIP" "TRAP" "TRIP" "TRAP"

and up to the hill to eat the sweet green grass
with his brothers.

The billy goats Gruff got sleek and fat
And that is the end of that!

The Great Big Enormous Turnip

by Alexei Tolstoy
Illustrated by Laurie Stein

Once upon a time an old man
planted a little turnip. The old man said,
"Grow, grow, little turnip,
Grow sweet!
Grow, grow, little turnip,
Grow strong!"

And the turnip grew up sweet and strong and big and enormous.

Then one day the old man went to pull it up. He pulled, and pulled again. But he could not pull it up.

The old man called the old woman. He said, "Come and help with the turnip."

The old woman pulled the old man.
The old man pulled the turnip. And
they pulled, and pulled again.
But they could not pull it up.

The old woman called
her granddaughter.
She said, "Come and
help with the turnip."

The granddaughter pulled the old woman. The old woman pulled the old man. The old man pulled the turnip. And they pulled, and pulled again. But they could not pull it up.

The granddaughter called the black dog. She said, "Come and help with the turnip."

The black dog pulled
the granddaughter. The
granddaughter pulled the
old woman. The old woman
pulled the old man. The old
man pulled the turnip.
And they pulled,

and pulled again.
But they could not
pull it up.
  The black dog called
the cat. She said,
"Come and help
with the turnip."

The cat pulled
the dog. The
dog pulled the
granddaughter.
The granddaughter
pulled the old
woman. The old
woman pulled the
old man. The old
man pulled the turnip.
And they pulled, and pulled again.
But they could not pull it up.
   The cat called the mouse.
He said, "Come and help
with the turnip."

The mouse pulled the cat. The cat
pulled the dog. The dog pulled
the granddaughter. The granddaughter
pulled the old woman. The old woman
pulled the old man. The old man
pulled the turnip. They pulled, and
pulled again.

And up came the turnip at last!

No Room

by Marilyn Souther
Illustrated by Philippe Béha

It was a cold, rainy day. An elephant was walking to town. He was so cold and wet. Just then the elephant saw a bus.

"If I get on that bus, I'll be warm and dry," thought the elephant.

The bus came to a stop, and the elephant got on.

A giraffe saw the bus. She was so cold
and wet.

"If I get on that bus, I'll be warm and dry,"
thought the giraffe.

The bus came to a stop.

"There's no room," said the elephant.

"I'm so cold and wet," said the giraffe.

"Well, maybe I could make room for you,"
said the elephant.

The giraffe got on the bus. Now there was
only a **little** room left in the bus.

A hippopotamus saw the bus. He was so cold and wet.

"If I get on that bus, I'll be warm and dry," thought the hippopotamus.

The bus came to a stop.

"There's no room," said the giraffe.

"I'm so cold and wet," said the hippopotamus.

"Well, maybe we could make room for you," said the giraffe.

"That's the last one," said the elephant.

The hippopotamus got on the bus. Now there was only a **very little** room left in the bus.

A kangaroo saw the bus. She was so cold and wet.

"If my baby and I get on that bus, we'll be warm and dry," thought the kangaroo.

The bus came to a stop.

"There's no room," said the hippopotamus.

"I'm so cold and wet," said the kangaroo.

"Oh, well," said the giraffe. "We'll make room."

"That's the very last one," said the elephant.

The kangaroo and her baby got on the bus. Now there was **no** room left in the bus.

A fly saw the bus. He was so cold and wet.

"If I get on that bus, I'll be warm and dry," thought the fly. So he flew into the bus.

Well, there was room on the bus for the elephant and the giraffe. There was a little room for the hippopotamus and only a very little room for the kangaroo and her baby.

But there was no room for the fly.

CRASH! SMASH! The bus fell to bits.

The elephant looked at the giraffe.
The giraffe looked at the hippopotamus.
The hippopotamus looked at the kangaroos.
Then they all looked at the fly.
"I have to go now," said the fly. And off he flew as fast as he could.

And the Rhymes Go On

Illustrated by Maryann Kovalski

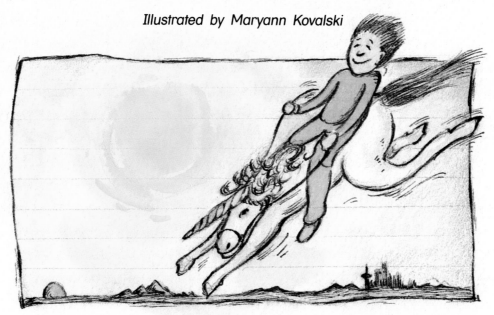

Rudy Rode a Unicorn

by Jack Prelutsky

Rudy rode a unicorn,
its mane was silver spun,
and west from Nova Scotia
they raced before the sun.

They soared above Toronto,
then north from Winnipeg,
they swooped into the Yukon
and found a golden egg.

Little Miss Dimble

by Dennis Lee

Little Miss Dimble
Lived in a thimble,
Slept in a measuring spoon.
She met a mosquito,
And called him "My sweet-o,"
And married him under the moon.

Chicken Forgets

MOTHER HEN: Chicken, I need your help. I want you to go berry hunting. I need a basket of wild blackberries.

LITTLE CHICKEN: I'd like to go berry hunting.

Adapted from the book by Miska Miles
Photographed by Ray Boudreau

MOTHER HEN: Take this basket and fill it to the top. Sometimes you forget things. THIS time, please, please keep your mind on what you are doing. Don't forget.

LITTLE CHICKEN: I won't forget. I'll hunt for wild blackberries.

STORYTELLER: He started across the meadow. And because he didn't want to forget, he said to himself over and over:

LITTLE CHICKEN: Get wild blackberries. Get wild blackberries.

STORYTELLER: All the way to the narrow river he kept saying:

LITTLE CHICKEN: Get wild blackberries.

STORYTELLER: Then the chicken heard the rusty voice of an old frog.

FROG: What are you saying?

LITTLE CHICKEN: Get wild blackberries.

FROG: If you're talking to me, you shouldn't say that.

LITTLE CHICKEN: Oh? What SHOULD I say?

FROG: Get a big green fly.

STORYTELLER: The chicken went on his way. And because he didn't want to forget, he said to himself:

LITTLE CHICKEN: Get a big green fly. Get a big green fly.

STORYTELLER: All the way to the pasture he said:

LITTLE CHICKEN: Get a big green fly.

Get a big green fly.

STORYTELLER: At the pasture, a goat pushed his head through the rails of the fence and twitched his beard.

GOAT: If you are talking to ME, you should NOT say, "Get a green fly." You should say, "Get green weeds."

LITTLE CHICKEN: Oh?

STORYTELLER: And on went the little chicken, past the pasture, saying:

LITTLE CHICKEN: Get green weeds. Get green weeds.

STORYTELLER: He said, "Get green weeds" all the way to the edge of the cornfield.

Get green weeds.

ROBIN: No, no. Berries are better. Follow me.

STORYTELLER: So the little chicken ran along the ground, following the robin's shadow, and he came to a beautiful patch of wild blackberries. The robin flew down and ate until he could eat no more. And the little chicken filled his basket with beautiful, shining wild blackberries.

Chicken forgets

STORYTELLER: He started home. Back he went, through the cornfield and beside the pasture fence by the river. He ate five berries. Across the meadow he went. And he ate three berries.

108

STORYTELLER: At home, the mother hen looked at the basket.

MOTHER HEN: You DIDN'T forget. You brought home blackberries, and the basket is almost full.

LITTLE CHICKEN: It's easy to remember when you really try.

MOTHER HEN: I'm proud of you.

STORYTELLER: And the little chicken was proud, too.

Deep in the Forest

by Brinton Turkle

The Magic Pot

Retold by Nicki Scrimger
Illustrated by Vesna Krstanovitch

Once upon a time there was a poor little girl who lived with her mother in a village that nestled between a forest and a river. One day when there was no more food in their house, the girl went into the forest to look for something to eat.

In the forest she met an old woman who asked, "What are you doing here all alone?"

"I'm looking for food," said the little girl. "My poor mother and I have nothing to eat."

The old woman pulled a pot out of a pocket in her cloak. "I will give you this magic pot," she said, "so you will not be hungry any more. When you want to eat, just say,

Snick, snack, snook
Cook, pot, cook!

and the pot will make you porridge. And when you have eaten your fill, just say,

Snip, snap, snop
Stop, pot, stop!

and the pot will stop cooking."

The little girl took the pot home, and whenever she and her mother were hungry, she made porridge in the magic pot.

One day, when the girl was out, her mother felt hungry, so she said,

Snick, snack, snook
Cook, pot, cook!

and the magic pot started to cook. It cooked and it cooked. It made porridge and more porridge.

The mother couldn't stop it because she couldn't remember the right words. She said *flip, flap, flop*

Flip, flap, flop!!

and *slip, slap, slop,* but the pot just went on cooking and didn't stop.

117

The porridge filled the pot and spilled
onto the floor. It filled the kitchen and spilled
into the street. It filled the street and spilled
through the village. Everyone ran
toward the river.

When the little girl saw the villagers running to escape from the porridge, she realized what had happened. She ran home and quickly called out,

Snip, snap, snop
Stop, pot, stop!

Immediately the little pot stopped cooking, and the villagers ate their way through the streets back to their houses.

If Wishes Were Horses . . .

by Pamela Mordecai
Illustrated by Suzanne Gauthier

If wishes were horses
my pony and I
would ride like the wind
to the ends of the sky.

We'd zip by the moon
and gallop past stars.
We'd go from Pluto
to Saturn and Mars.

If wishes were horses
my pony and I
would blaze like a comet
and light up the sky.

We'd speed past the sun
and kick up a trail
of silvery lightning
and shimmering hail.

If wishes were horses
my pony and I
would stop at the top
of the furthermost sky.

We'd sip some space-water,
and taste some star-grain,
and then we'd streak off
through the heavens again.

Meet Beatrix Potter

by Naomi Steiner
Illustrated by Karen Patkau

Do you know this rabbit? His name is Peter.
Beatrix Potter wrote about him in *The Tale of
Peter Rabbit,* and she painted pictures to
illustrate her story.

Beatrix wrote and illustrated many other stories about animals. This is how she came to write her books.

Beatrix Potter had lots of animal pets—

snails in a flower pot,

mice in a box,

bats in a parrot cage,

kittens in socks.

She also had a rabbit named Peter, a mouse named Hunca-Munca, and a hedgehog named Mrs. Tiggy-Winkle, who drank from a teacup.

Beatrix wrote letters to children she knew. She drew pictures of her pets and told about funny things they did.

One day Beatrix was writing a letter to a boy named Noel. She had no news about her pets. So she made up a story about four rabbits named Flopsy, Mopsy, Cottontail, and Peter. Noel and his family liked the story so much that she wrote more stories in other letters she sent to them.

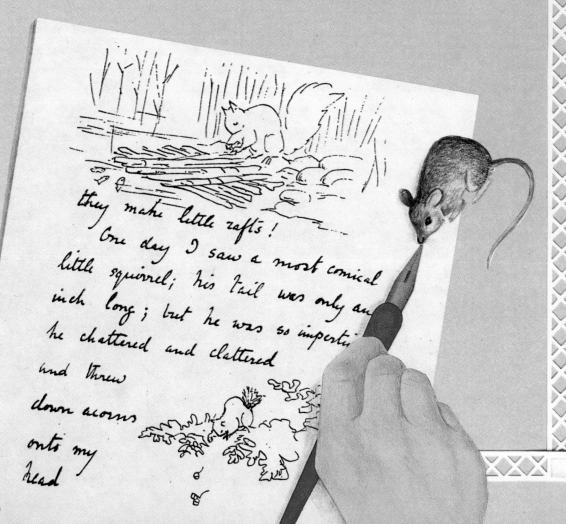

they make little rafts!

One day I saw a most comical little squirrel; his tail was only an inch long; but he was so impertin he chattered and clattered and threw down acorns onto my head

Then Beatrix had an idea. Perhaps other children would also like her stories. So she published *The Tale of Peter Rabbit* as a book. It became so popular that a publisher decided to turn all her stories into books.

Beatrix Potter went on writing and illustrating many more stories.

Which one do you like best?

Illustrations used
in unit openers:

Illustration from *The Mice and the Clockwork Bus* by Rodney Peppé, copyright © Rodney Peppé, 1986, reprinted by permission of Puffin Books, Penguin Books Ltd.

Illustration from *The Balloon Tree* by Phoebe Gilman, copyright © 1984 by Phoebe Gilman. Reprinted by permission of North Winds Press, 123 Newkirk Road, Richmond Hill, Ontario, Canada.

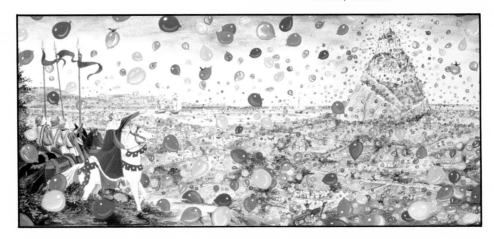